LBC MIDDLE SCHOOL
LIBRARY

ANAHEIM

RICHARD RAMBECK

THE HISTORY OF THE
ANGELS

CREATIVE EDUCATION

Published by Creative Education
123 South Broad Street, Mankato, Minnesota 56001
Creative Education is an imprint of The Creative Company

Designed by Rita Marshall
Editorial assistance by John Nichols

Photos by: Allsport Photography, Focus on Sports, Fotosport, Reuters, SportsChrome.

Copyright © 1999 Creative Education.
International copyrights reserved in all countries.
No part of this book may be reproduced in any form without written permission from the publisher.
Printed in the United States of America.

Library of Congress Cataloging-in-Publication Data

Rambeck, Richard.
The History of the Anaheim Angels / by Richard Rambeck.
p. cm. — (Baseball)
Summary: Highlights the key personalities and memorable games in the history of the team, once owned by Gene Autry, that played in Los Angeles until its move to Anaheim, California, in 1966.
ISBN: 0-88682-901-1

1. Anaheim Angels (Baseball team)—History—Juvenile literature.
[1. Anaheim Angels (Baseball team)—History. 2. Baseball—History.]
I. Title. II. Series: Baseball (Mankato, Minn.)

GV875.C34R355   1999
796.357'64'0979496—dc21   97-7130

First edition

9 8 7 6 5 4 3 2 1

In sunny Southern California, life is heavenly. The area is blessed with gorgeous weather, a booming economy, and a famous mouse . . . Mickey Mouse, that is. The beloved cartoon character makes his home in Anaheim, California, at Disneyland. With its fabulous rides, exciting shows, and marvelous attractions, Disneyland is where dreams have come true for people of all ages since 1955.

In such an otherworldly setting, you might expect to come across angels, and in this city they aren't hard to find. You merely have to go to The Big "A"—Anaheim Stadium—to discover the Anaheim Angels, the city's major-league baseball team.

An original member of the Angels, Ken McBride.

The Angels did not always make their home in Anaheim, however. When the ballclub debuted as an expansion team in 1961, it was based in Los Angeles as the American League answer to the National League's L.A. Dodgers. The team remained in L.A. until moving 30 miles south to Anaheim in 1966. At that point, the club was called the California Angels, a name it kept until 1997. In the franchise's nearly 40 years of history, it has seen many outstanding feats and accomplishments, but one prize has eluded the organization since the beginning—playing in the World Series. The Angels have never made it to baseball's Fall Classic, but the team's newest crop of stars have their sights set high. With young sluggers Tim Salmon, Darin Erstad, and Jim Edmonds leading the way, the Angels have a chance to see their own dreams come true in the magic city of Anaheim.

Gene Autry ("The Singing Cowboy") purchased interest in the new expansion team, the Los Angeles Angels.

ANGELS TAKE A CHANCE

Expansion teams are usually not expected to be very good, so when the Los Angeles Angels set a record for wins by a first-year team—70 in 1961—baseball fans everywhere were astonished. The club progressed even further the next year when it held first place as late as July 4, before fading to finish third. After the 1962 season, the team began to play more like the young team it was, finishing ninth in '63. But during those first three seasons, the Angels laid the groundwork for future success by developing young talents like Dean Chance.

Wilmer Dean Chance was a lanky lad who could throw a baseball with frightening velocity. This skill, combined with

Slugging right fielder Tim Salmon.

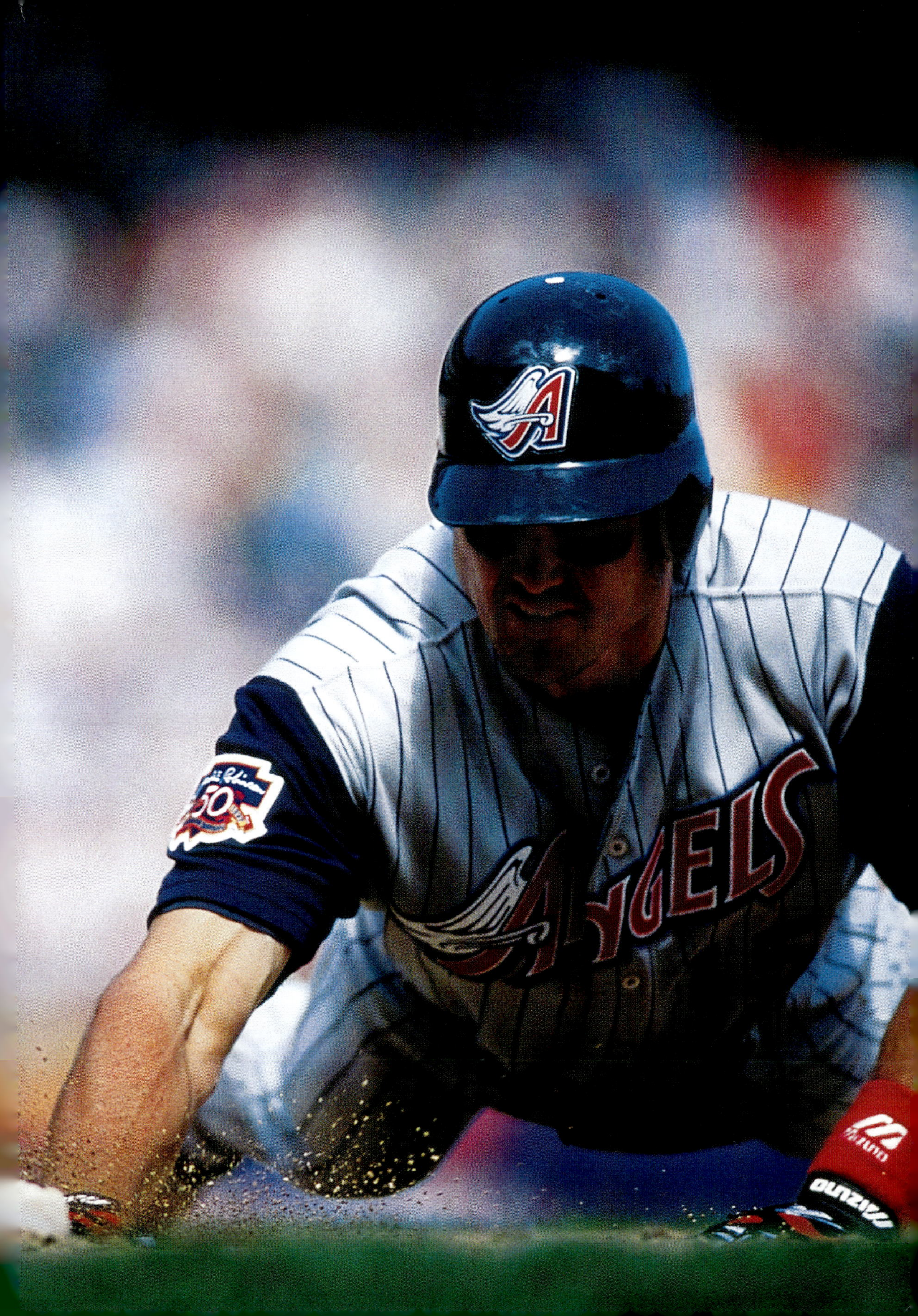
ANGELS

On May 5, tough lefthander Bo Belinsky threw the Angels' first no-hit game.

his more than occasional fits of wildness, unsettled hitters around the American League. In 1964, Chance's 20 victories, 11 shutouts, 207 strikeouts, and 1.65 ERA fueled the Angels' rise back above the .500 mark (82–80) and earned the young hurler the American League Cy Young Award.

Unfortunately for the Angels, Chance was destined to leave the team. The pitcher demanded a big raise from the Angels, but even famously generous owner Gene Autry, a former cowboy movie star, wasn't about to pay Chance what he asked. Chance then complained about the team's "penny-pinching" ways to the newspapers, the fans, and anyone else who would listen. Finally, his bragging and complaining made everyone, including his teammates, unhappy. In December of 1966, Chance was traded to the Minnesota Twins for outfielder Jimmie Hall, first baseman Don Mincher, and pitcher Pete Cimino.

Even without Chance, the Angels remained a fairly decent team. The main reasons were shortstop Jim Fregosi and second baseman Bobby Knoop. However, the Angels needed more quality pitching. So they traded for another young fireballer who was known to have occasional problems with control. That pitcher was Nolan Ryan.

THE RYAN EXPRESS STOPS IN CALIFORNIA

Ryan began his major-league career with the New York Mets in 1969, the year the amazing Mets won the World Series. But unlike other promising young Mets pitchers, such as Tom Seaver, Jerry Koosman, and Gary Gentry, the often-wild Ryan never found a home in New York.

Ryan struggled as a part-time starter until being traded to the Angels in 1972. When the hard-throwing right-hander landed in the American League, he flourished, winning 19 games for the Angels in his first year. He had a sparkling ERA of 2.29, and his 329 strikeouts easily topped the league. But Ryan also walked 157 batters, threw 18 wild pitches, and hit 10 batters.

Ryan's wildness actually became one of his best weapons. "Nolan Ryan is the only man in baseball I'm afraid of," said slugger Reggie Jackson.

"If he ever hits me," said Minnesota power hitter Harmon Killebrew, "I'll have him arrested for manslaughter."

In 1973, Ryan set a major-league record with 383 strikeouts. He also won 20 games and threw two no-hitters that season. "He's spectacular," said Herb Score, a pitcher for the Cleveland Indians during the 1950s. "With someone like Ryan, there is always the possibility of a no-hitter or a strikeout record. He is the kind of pitcher who draws fans. It's exciting to watch him."

It wasn't very exciting, however, for batters facing Ryan. Angels pitching coach Larry Sherry claimed that Ryan embarrassed hitters, "and they hate that. If you let him get a head of steam by the seventh inning, you can't hit him. You can't even see him."

Ryan had another great year in 1974, winning 22 games and throwing another no-hitter. During the 1975 season, however, he developed a sore arm that would give him trouble for several years. Despite the pain, Ryan threw another no-hitter in 1975, the fourth of his career, which tied a major-league record.

In the final appearance of his record-setting season, Nolan Ryan struck out 16 Minnesota Twins batters.

Angels ace Nolan Ryan.

The legendary Reggie Jackson.

1978

Angels outfielder Joe Rudi launched an unbelievable three grand slams during the season.

Unfortunately for the Angels, their level of success didn't match Ryan's. Despite a solid pitching staff, the Angels weren't able to dislodge the powerful Oakland A's and Kansas City Royals from the top of the American League West Division. What the Angels needed to put them over the top was a great hitter, and during the 1979 season, they made a key trade that landed them one of the finest in baseball—Rod Carew.

CAREW CRUISES AT THE PLATE

Carew, a first baseman, came to the Angels in a trade with the Minnesota Twins, and there was no doubt that he could hit. In fact, he had won the American League batting title seven out of 10 years between 1969 and 1978. He was known for his ability to adjust to all pitchers and all situations. Carew actually had several batting stances and relied on different ones, depending on how and where he wanted to hit the ball. "The man never wastes a time at bat," said Angels second baseman Bobby Grich. "I don't care if the score is 16–1 or 2–1. And he makes hitting look so effortless. You watch him, and you say to yourself, 'Boy, that looks easy.' Then you get up there and pop one up."

Carew believed the key to his success was his ability to remain loose at the plate. "I relax the upper part of my body," Carew said. "I don't squeeze the bat. If you do, you lose flexibility. When the pitch comes, I can direct my bat in many ways."

Carew had an immediate impact on the Angels, but outfielder Don Baylor had an even bigger impact. Led by Baylor, who won the American League Most Valuable Player award, the Angels won the AL West Division title in 1979, their first-ever division championship. Baylor, who had a league-leading 139 runs batted in, was one of several former Baltimore Orioles who keyed California's offense. Grich and third baseman Doug DeCinces were other ex-Orioles who had excellent years in 1979. To top it off, after winning the AL West, the Angels—and their ex-Orioles—had to face the Orioles in the American League Championship Series. Unfortunately for the Angels, Baltimore prevailed in the five-game playoff and advanced to the World Series.

Despite their success, the Angels and owner Gene Autry decided to make changes before the 1980 season. The biggest change was the trade of Nolan Ryan to the Houston Astros. Autry felt that Ryan, who was 16–14 in 1979, wasn't worth the price of a superstar. "Why, I can get two 8–7 pitchers for a fraction of what I'd have to pay him," Autry groused. The Angels' owner wasn't afraid to spend money, however, for players who could make the team a success. By the middle of the 1982 season, Autry had assembled a host of former American League Most Valuable Players: Fred Lynn (with Boston, 1975), Carew (Minnesota, 1977), Baylor (California, 1979), and Reggie Jackson (Oakland, 1973).

Led by these stars, the Angels stayed in contention for the AL West title all season. The home run was California's major weapon: Jackson hit 36, DeCinces clubbed 30, outfielder Brian Downing had 28, and Lynn hit 21. In addition, those four players accounted for 368 RBIs. The Angels also received great pitching from Geoff Zahn, who registered a

On September 25, Frank Tanana pitched a five-hit victory to clinch the Angels' first division title.

career-high 18 victories. Ken Forsch, Steve Renko, and Bruce Kison combined for 34 more.

The Angels wound up winning a club-record 93 games and also claimed the division championship. In the American League Championship Series, it appeared the Angels might give manager Gene Mauch his first pennant in his more than two decades of managing. California won the first two games of the best-of-five series against the Milwaukee Brewers, but both of those games were played at Anaheim Stadium. The Angels still needed one more triumph—but they didn't get it. The Brewers rallied for three straight victories in Milwaukee to win the series and advance to the World Series. The Angels returned to California as the first team to have blown a two-games-to-none lead in a league championship series.

California was unable to repeat as division champ in 1983, but Rod Carew put on a hitting display that will be remembered for a long time. The Angels' star hit above .400 for much of the season before tailing off in August and September. "The difference between this guy and the rest of us is that when we get hot, we go up to .300," Doug DeCinces explained. "When he gets hot, he goes up to .500." California center fielder Gary Pettis may have summed up Carew's ability best when he said, "Most guys hit when they can; he hits when he wants."

Carew continued to hit for a high average in 1984 and 1985. By the middle of the 1985 season, he stood on the threshold of a batting milestone—3,000 career hits. Carew got hit number 3,000 on August 6, 1985, at Anaheim Stadium. After the game, Gene Mauch praised Carew's work ethic as the main

Rod Carew set an Angels club record by hitting for a .339 average during the season.

The sweet-swinging Rod Carew.

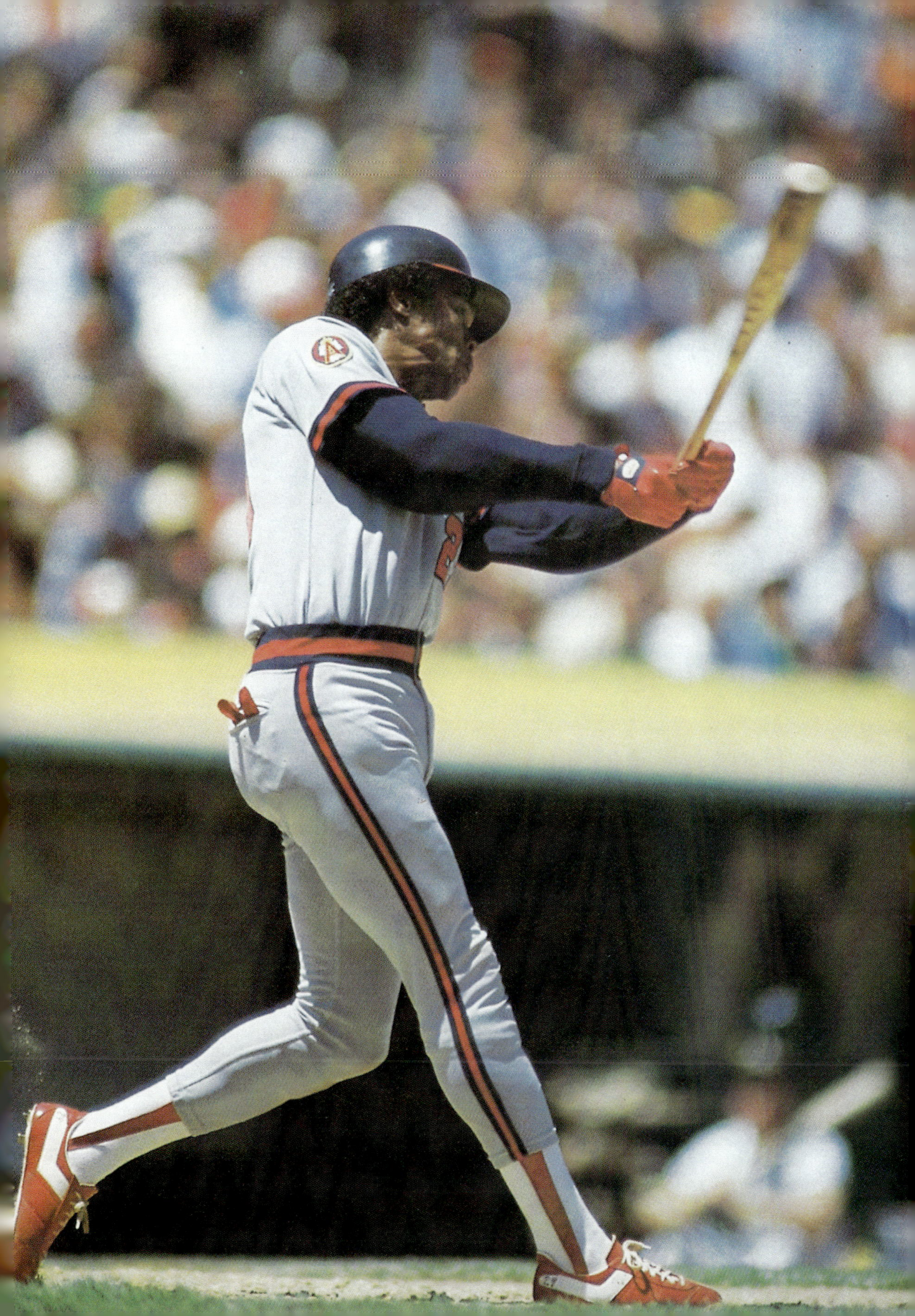

Gritty competitor Bobby Grich.

reason for him reaching his goals. "Rod was born with great hand-eye coordination, but he worked his rear end off to become a great hitter," Mauch said. "He has 3,000 hits, and he's gotten 100 in practice for every one of those, because he's practiced more than anyone you ever saw."

Carew's 3,000th hit was the last highlight of his Angels career. He would later go on to be inducted into the Baseball Hall of Fame in 1991, but at the start of the 1986 season, it was time for a new star to step forward at first base for the Angels. And oddly enough, it was Carew who helped develop the man who would take his place. The young player's name was Wally Joyner.

Angels slugger Reggie Jackson led the team in home runs with 25.

WELCOME TO "WALLY WORLD"

Joyner joined the Angels during the 1985 season, and one of his first teachers was Rod Carew. "I used to tell him, 'Here I am, helping you, and you're going to take my job!'" Carew joked. "Wally would give me one of his laughs and have this sheepish grin on his face. I told him, 'I'm only kidding, Wally. I can help you.' That's what we're all in this game for."

When the 1986 season began, Joyner was the Angels' starting first baseman, and even though Carew was no longer around to serve as teacher, Joyner had found a new instructor—Reggie Jackson. "I've worked with young players before, but this guy has taken advantage of my teaching more than anyone else," Jackson reflected. "He asks about everything. He wants to learn."

"He's told me about some of his stumbles," Joyner said,

Switch-hitter Chili Davis (pages 18-19).

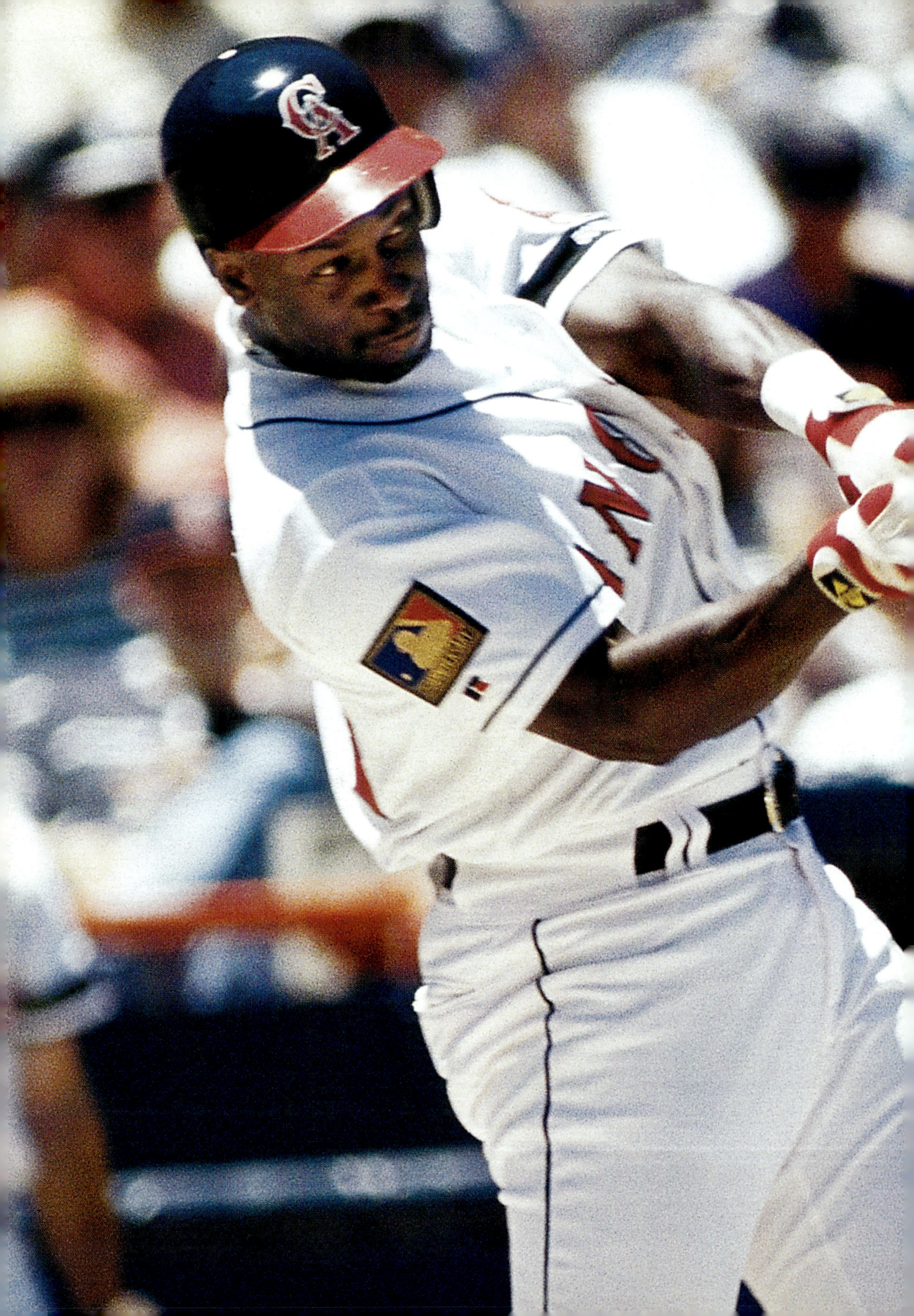

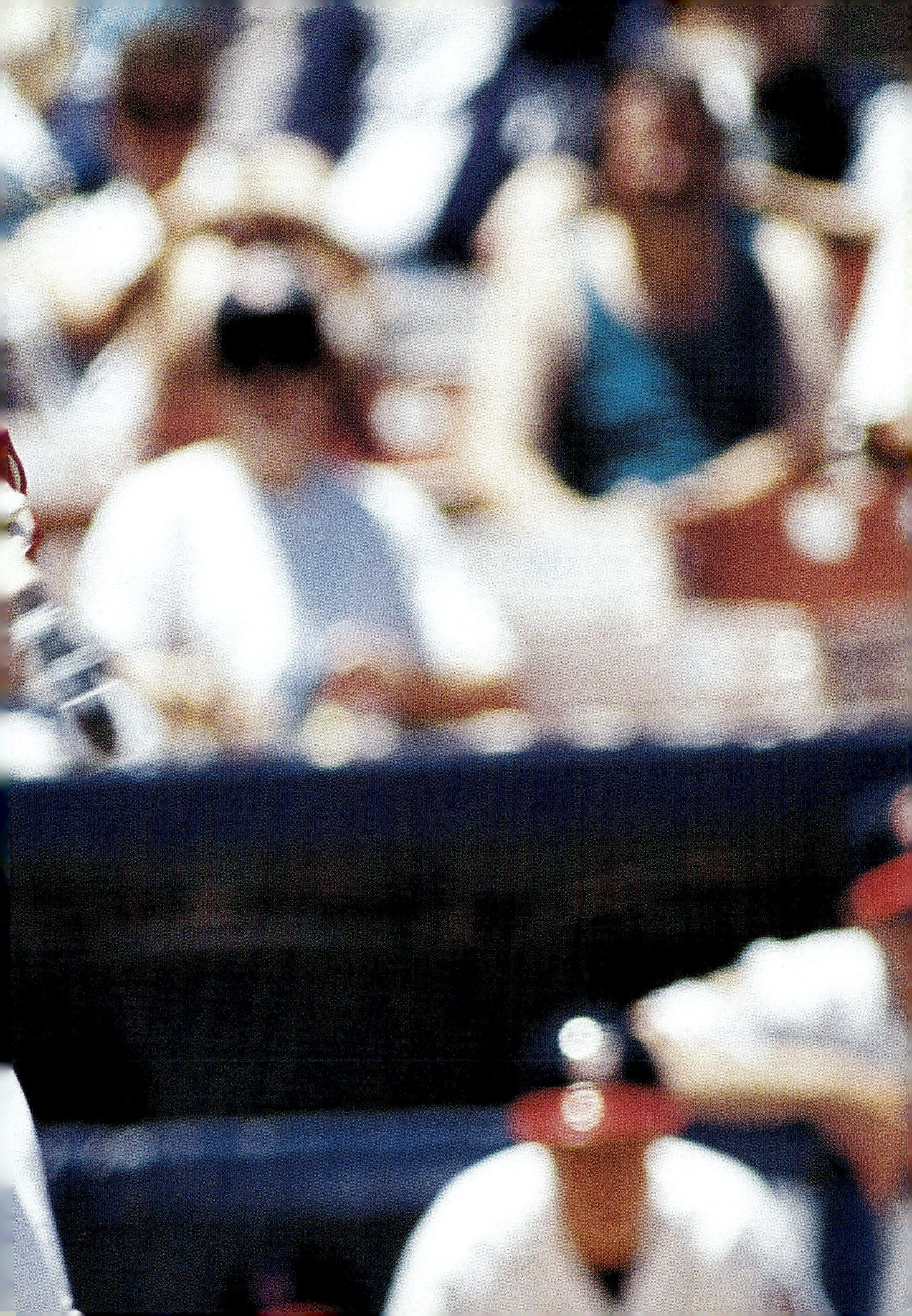

1985

New manager Gene Mauch guided the Angels to a 90–72 record, the second best in club history.

"and how to avoid them. We've talked about handling the good and the bad, the slump that is bound to come and sure to be magnified." Joyner, however, didn't have to worry about any slumps during the 1986 season. In fact, although he was not expected to have home-run power, Joyner immediately became one of the top long-ball hitters in the American League. "No one could have foreseen that this kid was going to hit 15 home runs in his first 37 games in the big leagues," Jackson said. "But I could see he had the tools." Joyner, however, didn't think he had the ability to use those tools. "I didn't expect to hit 15 [home runs] the whole year," he claimed. "I never think about hitting a home run. Sometimes I sit down, and it doesn't feel like I've ever hit one. I'm in dreamland."

Hard-throwing right-hander Mike Witt.

After watching Joyner hit, Angels fans began to think they too were in dreamland—or "Wally World," a phrase coined by one sportswriter. "He's such a good, all-American kid," explained Angels broadcaster Ron Fairly. "You want to stand next to him in a rainstorm because you know lightning won't hit him."

Led by the young Joyner and a cast of veterans, the Angels rose to the top of the American League West Division and stayed there. While California was winning, many of the players were reaching milestones. On May 14, 1986, Reggie Jackson hit his 537th home run to move past Mickey Mantle into sixth place on the all-time homer list. On June 18, pitcher Don Sutton became the 19th 300-game winner in major-league history. Sutton also achieved two other goals: he made 700 starts and pitched 5,000 innings.

By the end of the season, the Angels had reached a milestone as a team, winning the franchise's third division championship. It also seemed as if the club would make its first appearance in the World Series, as the Angels took a three-games-to-one lead against the Boston Red Sox in the best-of-seven American League Championship Series. In the fifth game of the series, nearly 65,000 California fans showed up at Anaheim Stadium to root the Angels to victory.

And victory seemed almost certain as California took a 5–2 lead into the top of the ninth inning. But then Boston player Don Baylor, a former Angel, slammed a two-run homer to cut the lead to 5–4. California manager Gene Mauch brought in ace relief pitcher Donnie Moore to halt the Red Sox. After allowing a base-runner, Moore faced Boston outfielder Dave Henderson with two outs and

On June 18, veteran pitcher Don Sutton became the 19th 300-game winner in major-league history.

Powerful catcher/DH Brian Downing.

quickly fired two strikes past him. But with the Angels one strike away from the World Series, Henderson broke their hearts with a two-run homer to give Boston a 6–5 victory. The series, now three games to two in favor of the Angels, shifted back to Boston, where the Red Sox won two straight to claim the American League pennant.

The loss was particularly hard on Mauch, who had managed 25 years in the majors without going to the World Series. The next year, Mauch promised to build a young team to replace California's aging stars. Unfortunately, the rebuilding process was too long for Mauch to take; he quit after the 1987 season. The job of developing such young players as outfielder Devon White, second baseman Mark McLemore, and shortstop Dick Schofield would fall on new manager Cookie Rojas. However, Rojas lasted only one season before being replaced by Doug Rader.

First baseman Wally Joyner led the Angels in base hits (167) for the second time in his career.

ABBOTT OVERCOMES OBSTACLES

When the 1989 season began, Doug Rader knew the team's success would be tied to how well his young pitching staff performed. The staff had plenty of talent—Kirk McCaskill, Chuck Finley, and a surprising left-hander named Jim Abbott. Born without a right hand, he still managed to become a top college pitcher and to star on the U.S. baseball team in the 1987 Pan American Games and the gold-medal-winning squad in the 1988 Summer Olympics. The Angels shocked the experts by letting the 21-year-old Abbott start the 1989 season in the major leagues. "My Pan Am Games teammates told me not to be nervous about the

1 9 9 1

Led by pitcher Chuck Finley and a new lineup, California completed a dramatic turnaround.

pros," Abbott said. "They said if you're a decent pitcher, the majors will force you to become a better pitcher."

There was no doubt Abbott could throw the ball, but could he field it? The answer was yes. Abbott had developed a technique of transferring his glove to his throwing hand after releasing the pitch. Then, if the ball was hit to him, he fielded it with his glove and, in one motion, pulled the mitt off of his throwing hand with his handless arm and threw the ball to the appropriate base. Abbott did this so smoothly that his fielding was actually considered a strength. "Anyone who approaches Jim as an oddity, believe me, is on the wrong path," Rader said. "Jim is the most unhandicapped person I know."

Abbott stayed in the Angels' starting rotation throughout the 1989 season, despite his lack of two hands, his inexperi-

All-Star pitcher Mark Langston.

ence, and the experts' doubts. "If he can look past his disability the way he has," said Milwaukee star Paul Molitor, "then my advice to batters who face him is that they better do the same thing." Abbott wound up the 1989 season with a respectable 12–12 record and a 3.92 ERA, both excellent marks for a rookie.

The 1989 season marked a big turnaround for the Angels, who had posted a losing record in 1988. Owner Gene Autry was so encouraged by the improvement that he spent $16 million to bring standout left-handed pitcher Mark Langston, a free agent, to the Angels for the 1990 season. Langston, considered one of the most gifted pitchers in the majors, joined a pitching staff already loaded with talent.

Jim Edmonds led the Anaheim club in home runs (33) and RBIs (107) for the season.

The Angels, however, did not have a banner year in 1990. Their 80–82 mark would be the first of five consecutive seasons at the .500 mark or below. At the center of the team's problem was a shortage of offensive production. But despite the disappointing records, Angels fans found a new hero to cheer for when Tim Salmon came upon the scene.

SALMON, ANGELS FIGHT UPSTREAM

At 6-foot-3 and 220 pounds, the talented Tim Salmon looks more like a football linebacker than a baseball player. And like a linebacker, the Long Beach, California, native has built a reputation as a big hitter. "Tim's one of those guys who, when they hit the ball, it makes a different sound," explained Angels shortstop Gary DiSarcina. "For most guys you hear the regular crack. When Tim hits one, it's like thunder. BOOM!"

Hard-hitting center fielder Jim Edmonds (pages 26-27).

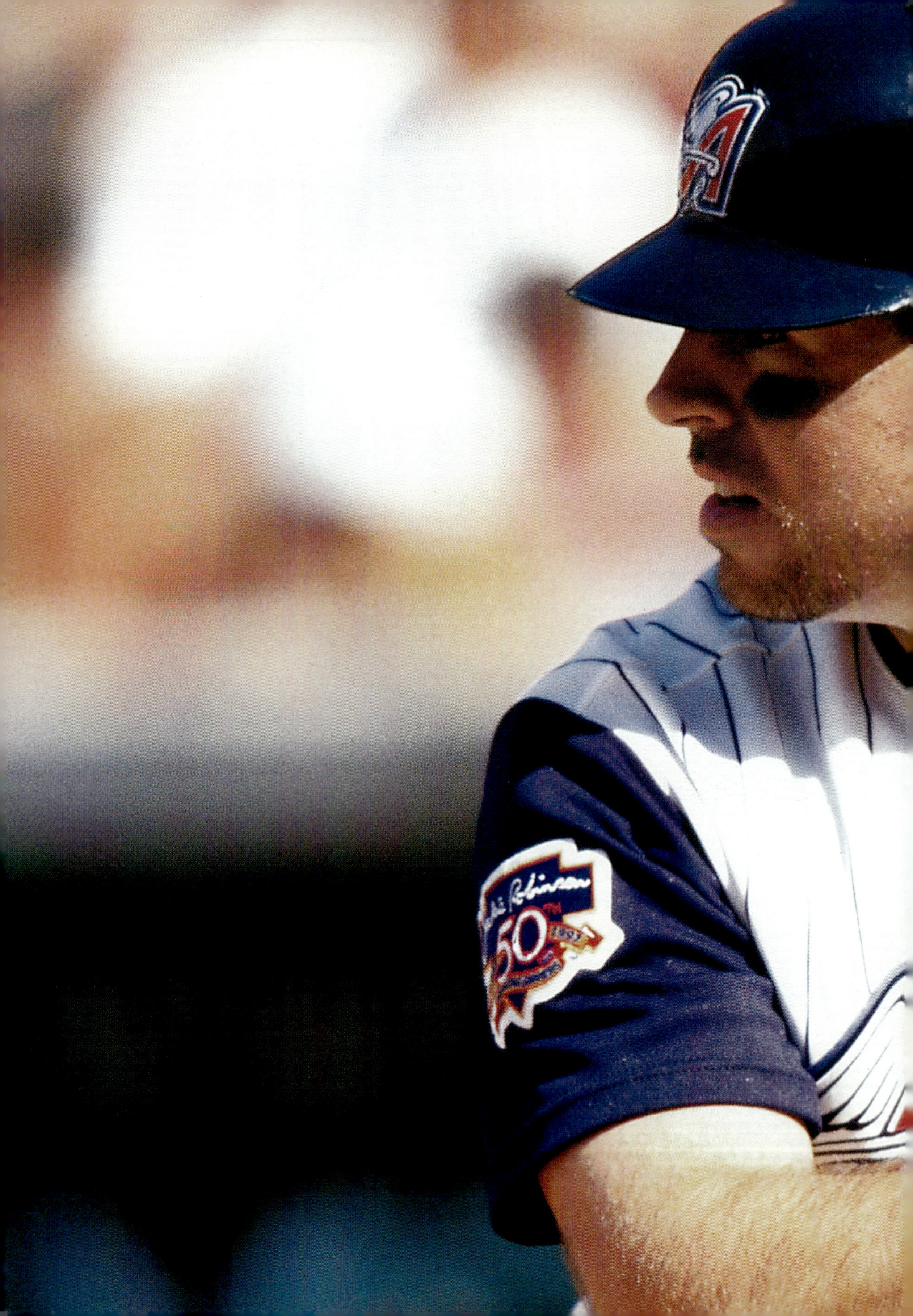
Robinson
50

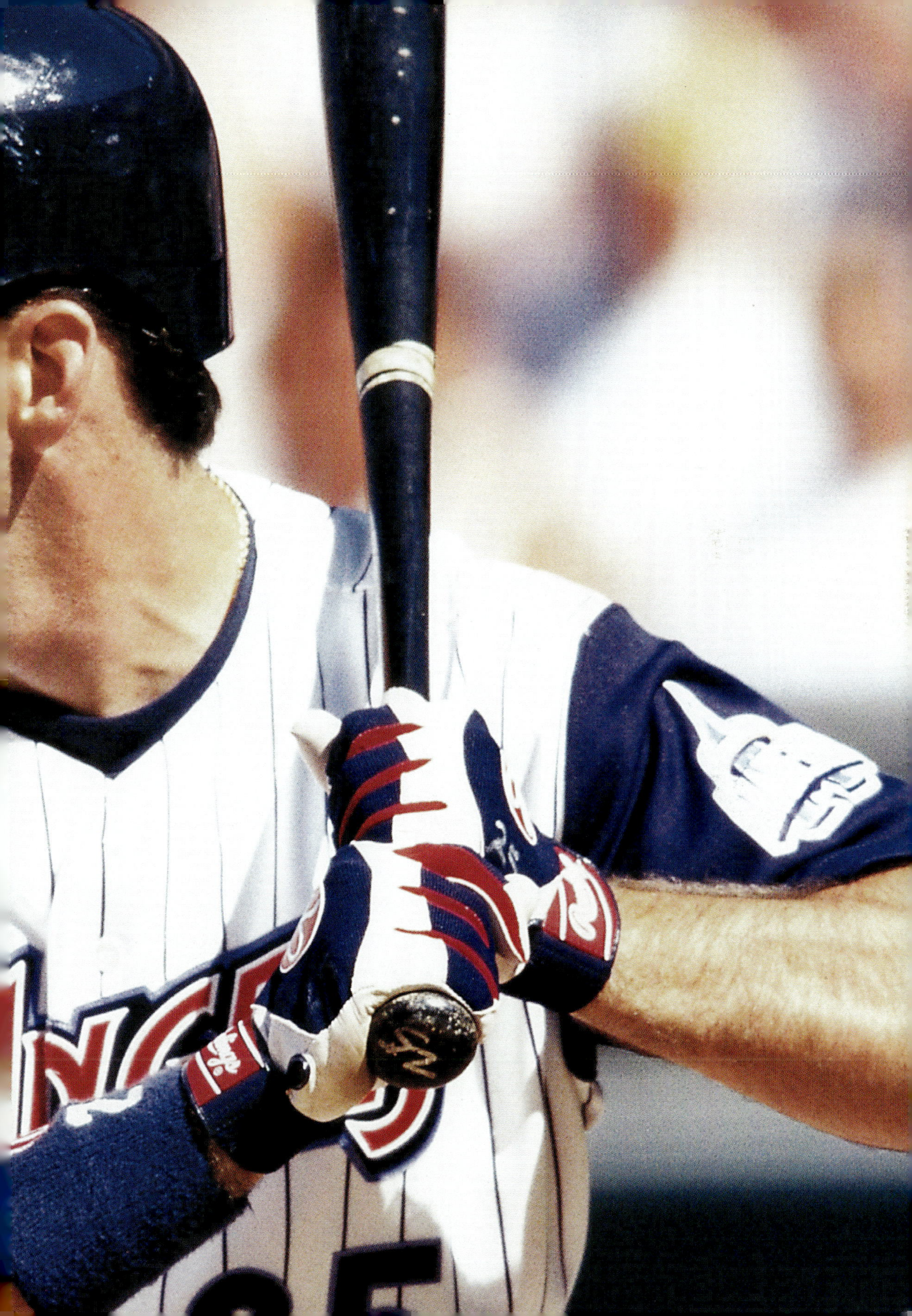

1995

First-round draft pick Darin Erstad was on the Cornhuskers NCAA Championship football team.

Salmon began unleashing thunderbolts full time for the Angels in 1993 when he crunched 31 homers, drove in 95 runs, hit .283 and won the American League Rookie of the Year award. The outfielder, a right-handed batter, had been one of the Angels' most prized prospects in the minors, and many teams tried to pry him away from the Angels with trade offers. But Angels general manager Buzzie Bavasi wouldn't hear of it. "This kid is going to be one of the guys who turns this team around," Bavasi explained. "All these teams are trying to trade us old mules for a young horse, and I ain't listening."

Salmon's rare combination of home-run power and high average allowed him to defeat pitchers in many ways. "I don't think of myself as just a home-run hitter," said the big right fielder. "I'll do whatever it takes to help us win. If it's a two-run single, I enjoy that just as much as a two-run homer." Salmon hit .330 in 1995, scoring 111 runs, belting 34 homers, and knocking in 105 RBIs. The Angels began to show improvement behind the hitting of Salmon and the strong pitching provided by Langston (15–7) and ace closer Lee Smith (37 saves). The club finished 78–67 in 1995, raising hopes for a big year in 1996. Unfortunately for Angels fans, the team would return to its losing ways. Despite a 30-homer, 98-RBI season from Salmon and 27 homers from third-year center fielder Jim Edmonds, the Angels faded to a 70–91 mark. "That was a tough year for all of us," explained Salmon. "But I think, through all the losing in '96, we learned some hard lessons about what it takes to win. This team has talent, and now's the time to show it."

Armed with the valuable experience of 1996 and a grim determination not to repeat it, the 1997 Angels stormed to a 66-50 record by early August and led the AL West by a half-game. Then disaster struck. Star pitcher Chuck Finley and sensational rookie catcher Todd Greene both suffered season-ending injuries, and sparkplug outfielder Tony Phillips was arrested on drug charges. The disheartened Angels went 18–28 the rest of the way to finish second, six games behind the Seattle Mariners. "It's a shame," said manager Terry Collins. "You try to plan for anything that can happen, but I would never have guessed this."

1996 — Garret Anderson became the first player in Angels history to get six hits in a game (Sept. 27 at Texas).

DISNEY HOPES TO SPARK MAGIC

One of the strengths of the Angels' franchise has always been stable, aggressive ownership. From the team's inception in 1961, owner Gene Autry provided unfailing support for his ballclub, both financially and emotionally. "I live and die with these guys," Autry said on many occasions. "I'm the Angels' biggest fan." In 1996, the 89-year-old owner made yet another winning move. Autry sold managing interest in the Angels to the Walt Disney Entertainment Company. "I'm very confident the Disney people will do everything in their power to continue our mission of winning a championship," said an emotional Autry.

With the transfer in ownership, the Angels have begun preparations for a winning future. With Tim Salmon, Mark Langston, and left-handed pitcher Chuck Finley forming a veteran nucleus, the Angels plan to develop young stars like Jim Edmonds and Darin Erstad. Edmonds, formerly known

Aggressive closer Troy Percival.

Versatile outfielder Garret Anderson.

Tim Salmon was looking good to lead the Angels in homers for the fourth straight season.

as a fence-crashing defensive whiz, came on like a summer storm in 1995, blasting 33 homers and driving in 107 runs. In only his second year in the majors, Edmonds displayed power that he had not shown in the minors or during his rookie season. "It's all about confidence and finally feeling comfortable at the plate for me," Edmonds remarked. "I've always had it in me—it was just a matter of bringing it out."

For Erstad, the pressures of being a big leaguer should not be a new experience. As the punter for the 1995 National Champion University of Nebraska football team, the left-handed outfielder/first baseman got used to the spotlight. Now baseball promises more opportunities for glory. After a midseason call-up in 1996, Erstad went on to hit .284 in 208 at-bats, and according to Angels manager Terry Collins, Erstad has the potential for greatness. "Darin's just such a gifted athlete," remarked Collins. "He has that football intensity, and with his speed and strength, it's going to be fun watching him develop into a star." With a solid combination of youth and experience, the Angels have assembled a team that should issue a strong challenge to the rest of the American League. "We're done learning; it's time to start winning," declared Edmonds. With that sort of confidence, it might not be long before these Angels earn championship wings.